I0734714

SIARAD

[sha-rad]

a Welsh verb

meaning

to talk,

speak

Praise for SIARAD

'Bettina Kaiser's distinctive black-and-white design and illustrations are a precise fit with both the form and the content of Reid's text, in an inventive collaboration between writer and artist.'
– Kerryn Goldsworthy, Sydney Morning Herald

'Reading SIARAD is to be led through the life, philosophy and imagination of a writer whose abilities extend far beyond the page. She is genre-fluid, crossing boundaries so effortlessly it makes us wonder why we thought those margins existed in the first place.'
– Rachael Mead, *The Application of Pressure, The Flaw in the Pattern*

'Caroline Reid's writing illuminates the mundane and the ordinary as spectacular and powerful.'
– Rosslyn Prosser, University of Adelaide

'SIARAD is the most enjoyable collection I've read this year … Absolutely recommended whether you think you like poetry or not.'
– Sarah Temporal, poet & performer

'I will leave a copy in my work bag that I take to and from the mine, kind of like *The Little Book of Calm* just in case I need a little reminder of what's important in life. It's amazing."
– Gary Holmes, FIFO worker

SIARAD the audiobook is extraordinary work, superbly delivered, set in a dazzling soundscape.'
– Ali Whitelock, the *lactic acid in the calves of your despair, and my heart crumples like a coke can*

Praise for Caroline Reid's poetry and performance

'Despite all the fun the author must have had arriving at its emotional core, this feels like a poem they had to write. It's urgent, tender and packed with lust for life.'
– Pascale Petit, judge, Mslexia Women's Poetry Award

'Caroline Reid's poem 'DEVOUR' made me laugh. More than once. I read it to my husband. He laughed. This is harder than it sounds. To write a genuinely funny poem is a difficult task, to write a genuinely funny political poem that doesn't shy away from puns I would've thought may be an impossibility. Let alone one that also blends thorough reference to Patrick White. 'DEVOUR' manages all of this.'
– Caitlin Maling, judge, Tom Collins Poetry Prize

'Wild, yet masterfully controlled, Caroline Reid's poem sings and it jars and is terrifying and haunting and every line triple-summersaults through the air and lands so precisely that if this were the poetry olympics, each line would score a perfect ten from each of the judges.'
– Ali Whitelock, judge, Woollahra Digital Literary Award for Poetry

'SIARAD is the hallmark of a woman who has the need to speak, and thankfully, also has something to say. The show is something like a punch in the stomach that you asked for, surprisingly painful in its intensity.'
– Emma Bedford, Artshub

'Reid admits she gets lost in the space between poems, and SIARAD is proof that it's those spaces that make her poems. It's serious stuff, being a serious poet, and yet she is incredibly personable and unpretentious in her delivery.'
– Heather Taylor Johnson, In Daily

'Reid's delivery of her words is masterful. It's no wonder she has twice been a finalist in the Australian Poetry Slam. She blends cadence with a conversational style that hits just the right balance. This is poetry of the best kind.'
– Alice Gorman, *Dr Space Junk vs The Universe*

'Stunning. Beautifully structured and lots of shades of emotions and experiences. If you love words and writing, this is just the perfect show.'
– Tracy Crisp, *An Evening with the Vegetarian Librarian, The Remakery, Pearls*

'As a performance poet, Caroline Reid is dynamic and adaptable, shifting gears in response to the space and the people who share it. Filled with warmth and knowingness, she is world/battle weary at times but not beholden to cynicism.'
– Steve Smart, *Melbourne Poets Union*

Caroline Reid

If you ask her where she's from, Caroline Reid will tell you that before Kalgoorlie, Western Australia, there was Bryngwran, North Wales (her mother's country) and Ballybofey, Ireland (her father's country). There was Nain and Taid and a lot of rain. And she will tell you that before she spoke English she spoke Welsh, most of it forgotten now but language and people are homes too and bits of both have crept into SIARAD. Before spoken word poetry she wrote plays. Currency Press published one of her scripts *Prayer to an Iron God*, not to wide critical acclaim. Her poetry and stories have been published by the likes of *Cordite Poetry Review*, *Red Room Poetry*, *Review of Australian Fiction*, *Spineless Wonders*, *Verity La*, *Quartet & Mslexia*. But, she will tell you, before poetry there was music. Her mother Margaret Eleanor Hugh was her first music teacher; her second was Kevin Bloody Wilson. Both have shaped the way Caroline uses language today. Margaret Eleanor Atwood says poetry uses the same part of the brain that is connected to music and maths, and it's not because Ms Atwood shares names with her mother that Caroline believes her. This book is not soundproof. It works best when read out loud. If she could she would recite the whole thing in Welsh but that's a work in progress. Caroline plays in multiple art forms: she recorded SIARAD as an audiobook with sound designer, Jeffrey Zhang, performs it as a spoken word theatre show and collaborates with filmmakers to make video poems, which have screened in international poetry films festivals. Most recently, Caroline was awarded the Mslexia Women's Poetry Prize and the Woollahra Digital Literary Award for Poetry. She lives in Adelaide on Kaurna country.

Bettina Kaiser

Bettina is a purple octopus orbiting earth.
(Should she not be in orbit, you can find her pottering around in her art studio or at her design desk. More at bkad.com.au or bettinakaiser.com)

The Poetry Book Awards
The international Poetry Book Awards is a Welsh-based annual award founded in
2020 for a collection of poetry written in English and published by independent,
small presses or self-published authors. In 2022 SIARAD was awarded second prize.

SIARAD
Caroline Reid

poetry & prose

for Margaret Eleanor Hugh

Spineless Wonders Publishing Pty Ltd
ABN 98156041888

PO Box 220
STRAWBERRY HILLS
New South Wales, Australia, 2012
shortaustralianstories.com.au

First published in 2020 by ES-Press
An Imprint of Spineless Wonders

Text © Caroline Reid
Design and illustrations by Bettina Kaiser
Editorial assistance by Matilda Gould

All rights reserved. Without limiting the rights under copyright reserved above, no part of this publication may be produced, stored in or introduced into a retrieval system, or transmitted, in any form or by any means (electronic, mechanical, photocopying, recording or otherwise), without the prior written permission of the publisher of this book.

Typeset in Artegra Slab
Printed and bound by Ingram Spark
ISBN 978-1-925052-49-7

Siarad, poetry & prose
Reid, Caroline

Distributed by NewSouth Books through Alliance Distribution Services (ADS)
Tel: +61 (2) 4390 1300
Email: adscs@alliancedist.com.au
newsouthbooks.com.au

A catalogue record for this work is available from the National Library of Australia

Contents

To touch and taste a comet

At five past six on a milky morning in November naked

from the waist down

dripping

perimenopausal sweat into my first black coffee of the day I wrote

    Be who you want to become

    but first know who you want to become

Jesus fucking Christ I hate it when I channel Gandhi at the crack

  of dawn

the grainy difficult dream in which I'm trying to fuck Atticus, a lover

who left twenty-four years ago

still prowling my mind like a starving shark.

I want to become Tyler Durden without the mental illness but

the only club I belong to is the

  one-parent-dead-the-other-has-dementia club

but

I am trying to become ambitious so

I read a story in a back issue of New Scientist

    To touch and taste a comet

and am so underwhelmed by the picture of Comet 67P's bulbous
    shape
marked in cheap primary colours
            where sunlight falls
                or not
I could never guess Comet 67P is a wildly alien landscape with only
a few spots safe for landing
and I think Jesus fucking Christ
there's a metaphor for life.

Well, the world is a kind of nothing place and
I am like a rubbish pile inside and yet
To touch and taste a comet is written in font more
        bewildering
        elegant
                than any comet
                    it makes me feel something I have
                    no language for
that may be out of my reach forever.

I am striving to become brave and write good poetry, which means

I must write Jesus fucking Christ and Atticus three times in this poem
    because

three is the number of betrayal, Atticus

oh, Atticus

who gave me a garlic press when you left back in '94.

Made in Switzerland, she has forty holes where the flesh worms out
    in a pleasing way.

You held her higher than a trophy and said

> *This garlic press is a metaphor*

while I hid behind cheap red wine not knowing what the garlic press
    was a metaphor for

and feeling too scared

> sad

> bored

> stupid

> to ask.

See, I imagined my intelligence as tooth-sized back then

> shrinking

> to flea-sized

in the sober days with a surface as fragile as fresh fallen dandruff.

Some days the garlic press reminds me of a speculum

reminds me how careless we were back then

how you lost your mother as sudden as a gunshot

how seven years later my father went

   (twin towers fallen)

how that house with its glimpse of the dirty river from the enormous

 red-bellied bathroom

got demolished

but the garlic press has lasted.

Sure, her hinge is a little loose but she remains what she is

without striving to become something

         else.

In the end I want to be useful

  hopeful

  kind

but ending is always the difficult part because

fucking is not a metaphor and

we were always somewhere in between

  Atticus and I

    his name

    always too much on my tongue

our pain

always too much in my belly

which is almost definitely a metaphor but
some days I still don't know what –

Like my mother, I would like to be forgetful

but my dreams won't let me

I want to touch and taste the comet.

Who likes custard?

Donald Sutherland had been watching me. He had dandruff in his white Ned Kelly beard. He knew my birthday, said it was the same as his. He offered me a Tic Tac. I took three. People came and went. He asked me what I like about trees.

'Their shade?' I said, squinting up at him.

He said he had been watching me for quite some time, from the library, behind green-tinted windows. Donald Sutherland in the Tea Tree Gully library, watching me watching him. Life's a funny thing.

Don and I walked for a while before we stopped in the shade of a tree in the park. We sat together on a bench. He had been talking the whole time. Maybe that's his way of filling the emptiness. I smoke. Don talked about his wife, who is slowly going insane.

'We found out the day before Christmas,' he said. 'All the family were over. I said to my wife: Cry now. There there, dear, cry it all out.' He told me he woke early the next day, before the fuss of Christmas morning had begun, children still dreaming of Santa and reindeer; not even the birds were up. The Don nursed his coffee and padded around the kitchen. He said the sky looked grey, diseased. He wished it was over already. That was eight years ago.

I was bored with Don's story by then and wished he would go cry his blue eyes out somewhere else.

While Mick and I are having breakfast I tell him that Donald Sutherland breathed into my scarf, grabbed my crotch with his grandfather hands – wrinkled but still strong and sexy – bent me over the park bench and we did it in the shade of a tree opposite the Tea Tree Gully library.

Mick says, 'Who's Donald Sutherland?'

I tell Mick stories like this to make myself sound more interesting. We both know they're not true but I'm afraid if he really knew who I was he would leave. There's blandness in me. It's like cheap custard. Smoking helps.

Breakfast with Mick is coffee and toast and him wiping crumbs off the kitchen table. I like to shake cinnamon on the floor just to watch him sweep it up.

'Donald Sutherland is another way of saying cinnamon,' I say. Cinnamon makes me think of Baghdad in a fairytale, women selling brightly coloured scarves with gold trim, children stealing dates and dried fish, creating chaos.

As we run out the door, down Paradise Road to catch the bus to work, I tell Mick my great-grandfather was an Afghani trader.

'This has got to stop,' he says, freezing on the spot with his hands on his hips. That's his way of making a point.

The B53 comes and goes.

'I like being late,' I say. 'Makes me feel like Jesse James, Steve McQueen. I think I'll photocopy my arse first thing when I get into work today.'

'This, this.' Mick waves his arms about. He looks like Buddy Holly in those glasses. 'No more Afghani traders, Steve McQueen. No more Donald Sutherland.'

I know what he means. It must get tiring. But he does not want the alternative, believe me. Bland custard? I don't think so. He has to trust me on this. Besides, he's got his sweeping, the Don has got his talking, and I swear to God that is Christopher Walken waving to me from the bus stop.

The always unbalanced washing machine

the Libra girl has gone to Japan gone. the dirty-girl-with-little-boy girl just disappeared. the soft-crazy-aqua girl, ahead-of-her-time-and-wise girl thinks you're wrong but she will sleep-sleep-sleep with you. the red-head kissed you once then found new friends. the paisley-wearing tall girl, the never-broke-your-heart-but-made-you-sad girl is gone. now the girls are all gone swing your blank blue eyes back and forth, so wide-eyed wise one who comes down the hall. swing your eyes, blink-swing your eyes. away they go spinning across morning-night, skip-shifting night. away you go shifting like the fast hot-coloured telly-vision tunnel lights, bright and around to you. your good heart lifts swelling grey. your heart your eyes your clear conscience see rude women on the phone and in the hall. the landlady says this cat on the doorstep sounds like a child and where's my rent? the soft-crazy-kiss-time-Libra all gone just like that washing machine becomes you

Murder Girl gets wired

Tapping at windows on the city south road Murder Girl is looking for Poor Poor Boys who don't respect the law, whose jocks don't match their socks, whose mama's curtains don't match the carpet, whose cul-de-sacs ain't safe, only yesterday a child got hit in reverse, o the price and the dread and the price and the shame of it. wot du we du about this place? Girls and boys drenched in hectic religion with smelly haircuts, shady lounge rooms, thinking about future, three minutes to zero, bank accounts, super-duper, now there's a life. Murder Girl wired is like opal in the desert, what a girl, what a shake-up, loving with the Dirties, that's where she wants to be, with Poor Poor Boys being gawked at and talked at and she, the Night Princess, in love with night love, is all for cigarettes if they prove she can't win.

Highway One

The husband was half-asleep when he felt the car slowing. He opened his eyes to see a tall man in a funny hat rushing towards them, arms hanging loosely as if they didn't belong to the running body. 'There's a sight for sore eyes,' he said.

The tomboy giggled into her hand when the man squeezed in beside her. He was like a skyscraper in the car, shoulders wide, hat kissing the ceiling.

He is all solid lines, thought the wife, watching him in the rearview mirror. 'It's warm to be out,' she said. 'I'd turn the air-con on for you but it's broken, worse luck. D'you want a drink, luv? Some water? Get him some water.'

The man in the funny hat looked puzzled. The tomboy stabbed a finger at her mouth. 'Glug-glug-glug,' she went. The man touched his cracked lips, then smiled ferociously. His teeth were almost green. The wife glanced at her husband, who grunted and passed back some water in an old Coke bottle. The man bowed his head in thanks, his hat clunking the faded ceiling each time he lifted his chin.

'Glug-glug-glug,' went the tomboy as the man guzzled the lukewarm water.

The wife pulled out onto the highway. The car lurched its protest as she climbed through the gears.

'Where you off to, luv?'

The man spoke while pointing to a glossy mirage on the dead-straight road.

'What's he saying, Mum?' asked the tomboy.

'I don't know, sweetheart. I think it's Russian.'

'Turkish,' said the husband.

'I'm ten,' said the tomboy. 'This is my little brother. He's a sissy.' She punched him in the arm to prove it. The sissy punched her back.

'Stop it,' said the wife, who looked accusingly at her husband. They were his words alright. His son was a sissy. The husband knew he wasn't supposed to have favourites, but bollocks to that.

'He smells of onions,' said the sissy, pinching his nostrils shut.

The man in the funny hat lifted a cheek and farted.

'Gross,' said the sissy.

The tomboy pretended to choke. The husband laughed out loud. The man grinned.

'Don't encourage him,' said the wife. 'Where – are – you – from?' she asked, enunciating her words.

The man ruffled the tomboy's hair. She leant away from him, into the sissy's chubby arm.

'Get off me,' said the sissy, squeezing himself as far as he comfortably could into the car door.

'I'm – from – Australia,' said the wife, louder this time. She pointed at her husband. 'He – from – England. And – you?'

They all turned to look at the man, who wiped sweat from his eyes.

'Owstralia.' He nodded. 'Owstralia.' His hat thumped the ceiling.

'Gawd, you'd think he'd at least learn the basics,' said the husband, winding down the window. Hot, noisy air rushed into the car. 'He's probably simple.' The sissy heard sour words fly out of the car into the blue.

'I bet it's lovely, where you're from.' The wife smiled into the mirror but the man in the funny hat wasn't looking her way. 'What about an orange, luv? Give him an orange.' The man accepted the orange, making curious noises like he'd never seen one before.

Instead of eating it, he threw it from one big hand to the other, as if the casual fling of fruit might loosen the stifling atmosphere in the car.

The tomboy wriggled and huffed. The sissy breathed through his mouth and used a greasy finger to draw ninjas on the window. The husband half-turned towards the back seat, pretending to look at scenery, which was just an unremarkable plain with some tufts of grass, when what he was really doing was keeping an eye on the stranger's tanned thigh touching his daughter's leg. 'No luggage?' he said looking into the man's face. 'No water?'

The man held the orange still and squinted out the window.

The husband squeezed his daughter's leg. 'We'll stop soon,' he said to his wife.

The man gestured at a road sign up ahead.

'I think he wants to get out,' said the tomboy.

The wife took it to mean the man in the funny hat didn't like them, and she had trouble with that. Maybe her husband was right, maybe he was simple. The car crunched to a standstill on the gravel shoulder. The husband got out first.

'I'll drive now,' he said.

They left the man standing in the thin shadow of a green road sign.

'He forgot his orange,' said the tomboy when they'd gone a way up the road.

The wife peeled the orange. It was warm and sweet.

Colonisation

exit

Sharper and sharper it grew until altogether scissors threw gold and responded with climate. Baby's bottle did hum glue it. Fire and rubber prettied the Horror Show. How are the rules of butter shoved over? On a candlewax brass plate, he said, fetching frames and fossils divine, Brits and bread-apple kisses. Drag them up by the hairs of their dreamy sticky drains, that's the engine, sweet toots. Clay acquires imaginary swearing skills, sliming like a paintball in red dirt. The stamp sucker aches, wants management fees and coke with reasonable resistance to the worm. The Horror Show limes, nose all forest-clutter smallpox, a peppermint will to live and spare words, her red knees klunking. Sod Purple Out.

Satisfied

A cat creeps over the dark city roof of Bray's Antiquarian Bookshop, where each night after shutting up shop Carah and Bryce Bray get together in the back kitchen. Dressed in Bubble Wrap and silk stockings, Carah sits on the old school chair while her husband, a man with a fetish for women in Bubble Wrap and silk stockings, writhes and moans at her feet. He paws her legs and jams his fingers into the bubbles, his breath coming harder with each bubble burst; and she responds by crushing her heel into his mouth until his gums bleed, until he weeps, until he is satisfied.

At first Carah found her husband's fetish charming, almost amusing, but three years into their marriage she is keen for the straight sex they had when they first began courting.

'Even on weekends?' says Bryce.

'Especially on weekends.' Carah scratches the pimply rash on her torso, an allergic reaction to the polyethylene.

'But I've no interest in vanilla sex,' Bryce pouts.

'Then I refuse to play dress-ups any longer.' Carah gives away the Bubble Wrap and stockings to St Vinnie's and refills her cupboards with polyester slacks.

The cat continues to creep over dark city roofs.

Bryce decides to pay another woman to meet him at the Exalted Moon Resort, a woman who takes his money but mocks his fetish.

'You are boring,' she says.

He pays her more.

'You are unboring,' she says, and wears the Bubble Wrap.

For a while, Bryce is satisfied.

Carah satisfies herself by reading *An Introduction to Freud* and suddenly she figures it out. Her husband's fetish is the result of unresolved childhood trauma. However, having a great deal of unresolved trauma herself, she decides this is still no excuse for his bad behaviour and she finds herself frequently shouting and swearing at him: She is sick of his parasitic nature, his pointy fucking beard which he strokes all the time, and – of course – that stupid Bubble-Wrap-and-silk-stocking fetish. But Carah wasn't a born shouter and when she finds Bryce in Military History, kneeling between overstuffed bookshelves, satisfying himself on the stockinged legs of a customer who also appears to be satisfied, she stops shouting and holds this information tightly and quietly inside.

The following week, Carah hires a creative writing student to work in the bookshop. The student isn't backward in coming forward and quickly reveals he has a thing for older women who dress in polyester slacks. He also reveals his split penis, which can reach places in Carah she never knew existed. Finally, the student reveals he is writing a novel, a magic realist story whose main character is a giant bug.

'I'd be delighted,' says Carah, when the student asks if she wouldn't mind reading each chapter and giving him feedback. But after

finishing the long chapter in which the albino bug lives for a year
in Berlin on a government fellowship from the Ministry of Arts,
composing an Opera by plucking the hairs on his legs, Carah loses
interest. And who can blame her. Things get tense when the student
begins to identify with his protagonist and refuses to kill bugs in
the bookshop, even when they munch through rare collector's items
and Carah loses money hand over fist. She threatens to sack him. The
student suggests that instead of sacking him she might dress him in
Bubble Wrap, tie him to the old school chair and stroke his stockinged
legs until he is satisfied.

Carah can't believe what she's hearing.

Nor can Bryce, who is over the Exalted Moon and takes the student
up on his offer. This is the last straw. Carah bequeaths the failing
bookshop to St Vinnie's. The student moves to Berlin and, having
nothing better to do, Bryce tags along. They cruise gloomy German
bookshops and co-author a magic realist memoir detailing their
experiences called *Bubble Wrapped in Berlin*. Nobody buys it.

Back in the bookshop, Carah finds a book of spells, turns herself
into a cat and lives a long and happy life in the bookshop's kitchen.
She writes great works of literature by day and creeps over dark city
roofs at night. In this way, she is satisfied.

(Activism)

This is not a fairytale.

Berri really is a place, where oranges grow
But in the years of the Millennium drought
orchards were ripped out
You could see mature trees robbed of possibility
on the soft shoulder of the highway
Thick roots of trees
     clawing the air
     gasping for water
     begging for their lives
People committed suicide
and Berri's never been the same
And me?
I am ashamed

  (bcs I saw it on the television

  and did nothing)

It was breaking news

And I did nothing.

Now I stand here reciting poetry

so you might recognise the apathy inside of me

and it goes something like this –

       The drought went on for such a long time

       but what can you do? Empathy has a shelf life.

       And to be a fruit grower in South Australia

       is to live with the risk of drought.

       And oranges are not the only fruit, right?

Now, if you go down to The Riverland

to smell the sweet scent of oranges

you may hear the voices of women calling kids home at dusk

and you may wonder –

How do these Riverland people live

with the fear of drought
with the sharp taste of grief
with the memory of the dead knitted into their days.

And you may ask yourself
Or, you could ask them –

Has drought changed you?
Made you stronger?
Knowing the bad days are not over?
Knowing you are at-risk people
on an at-risk river
in an at-risk town?
And knowing that what is left of Berri's oranges
   get crushed
   and squeezed
   and squeezed and juiced
   and juiced and bottled
   in a faraway land

Just like in a fairytale.

A ceremony to commemorate the golden jubilee of Queen Elizabeth II

In glorious southern heat she wears cotton gloves,

white, to protect her hands.

And sensible shoes won't spear holes in the soft lawn sea.

While she watches a dark-skinned boy dance for her

to the didgeridoo drone

the clack of sticks

white paste on desert skin

soles like tough pads

like Emu
        like Kangaroo,
a trickle of sweat travels between her breasts.

Like Snake he flies fast but the grass here is not the same
and his toes get a little stuck.
When he tripped on some invisible thing
she was seen to gasp and press white cotton to her bosom
        thumb over thumb
before the wooden tube throat rattled feverishly
sticks chattering a language
like Cicada
like Blood at high tide to bear him up
and so he finished big and wide.

When the willy-willy came to carry the whole mob home
he was found teaching the old lady
in her big white shiny bathroom
where she peed after the ceremony
how to dance Crocodile.

5 drunk moons in Darwin

moon pig lazy
over a ping-pong world
sautés the sky

she likes to dance
naked and drunk
moon in hand

they say these two danced together
moon the fire
woman the bloody open pod

moon holds a rose between its teeth
sings karaoke on the corner
why are you standing alone?

she has a special skill
she knows how to capture
moon burps

Jason's advice

you know, miss

if you want to get married

and get kids

just go into town

you find yourself one man there

get married

get kids

very easy, miss

the kid

ravishing in frost and a tinkle of jewels
the kid sings at night
it makes her feel less like a tweet
more like a blue-tongued skink slipping over pinballs
or a transvestite gallivanting
in a stew of possible

she sings for hops
in a razzle-dazzle-black-money club
where the layout of gin rushes
like bored thoughts through blood
she sings:
Jelly bounces high when it's raspberry wet

she pauses. like lightning.

a hung whaler moon plaits its diacritical crown.

the kid owns all the parties of tomorrow
and tomorrow and tomorrow
yet she dreams of being space-bound
in some delicate steel monster
serenading stars
shredding ice hearts into milk

Sister

On the walk home the other day
I spied a sign at the old Works Depot:

DANGER
Fragile & Brittle Roof
Use Crawl Boards

I believe in signs, I do
I believe signs that warn and instruct
are clues
to the poems we're struggling with.

Have you ever tried to count the signs
on a stretch of urban road?
It's an impossible task.
There are so many
each one a work of art
that is unseen daily.

Sister
we have unseen so much.
Sister
I have unseen you
and you would rather run into a road train
than run into me.

The last time I saw you
I wasn't generous.
I wasn't kind.
Being in your kitchen was like
being in the room with loss.
Your face was a tangled ball of string.
I didn't recognise you.
You may as well have been a dead camel
keeled over in a dry creek bed
maggots writhing your eye sockets
roots of thorny bush tangling your mouth.
I heard David Attenborough narrate your body's time-lapse decay:
And of course the saddest part is
he said

in that clipped, wet accent.

But how could he know

what the saddest part is?

Sister

You are nastier than me.

A bitter little girl living under

a fragile and brittle roof.

But would you look at me go –

What a Fucking Bitch!

Not willing to give over

                not even in a poem.

Am I so sad I can't even find the crawl board?

I know I'm crazy when it comes to metaphors.

I love them more than I love you.

Love.

Isn't she a difficult mistress?

Ignore her and she turns faster than a bushfire.

Her borders become unstable

her home is not a given

her wound howls like a defeated mountain.

Sister

I gave up fighting for you years ago.

Gave up trying to understand you too.

And like you.

You are not my friend on Facebook.

Love though, different story.

Was there love when you led the way up the mountain

as older sisters do?

I recall the story of Innana visiting her older sister, Ereshkigal,

in the Underworld.

In the biggest catfight in history, Ereshkigal killed her younger sister

then hung her corpse to rot

on a meat hook.

You taught me how to fight, Sister

then I gave up fighting for us.

I dreamt you so small and fragile

I could pour you into my pocket like sand.

I dreamt I left you to drown on the shore of a strange river

and after your death I was the one to tend you

laying your body down in a basket of berries

placing you safely among the rushes

and as you slept the unseen sleep of the dead

I spied on you

from my cold and distant moon.

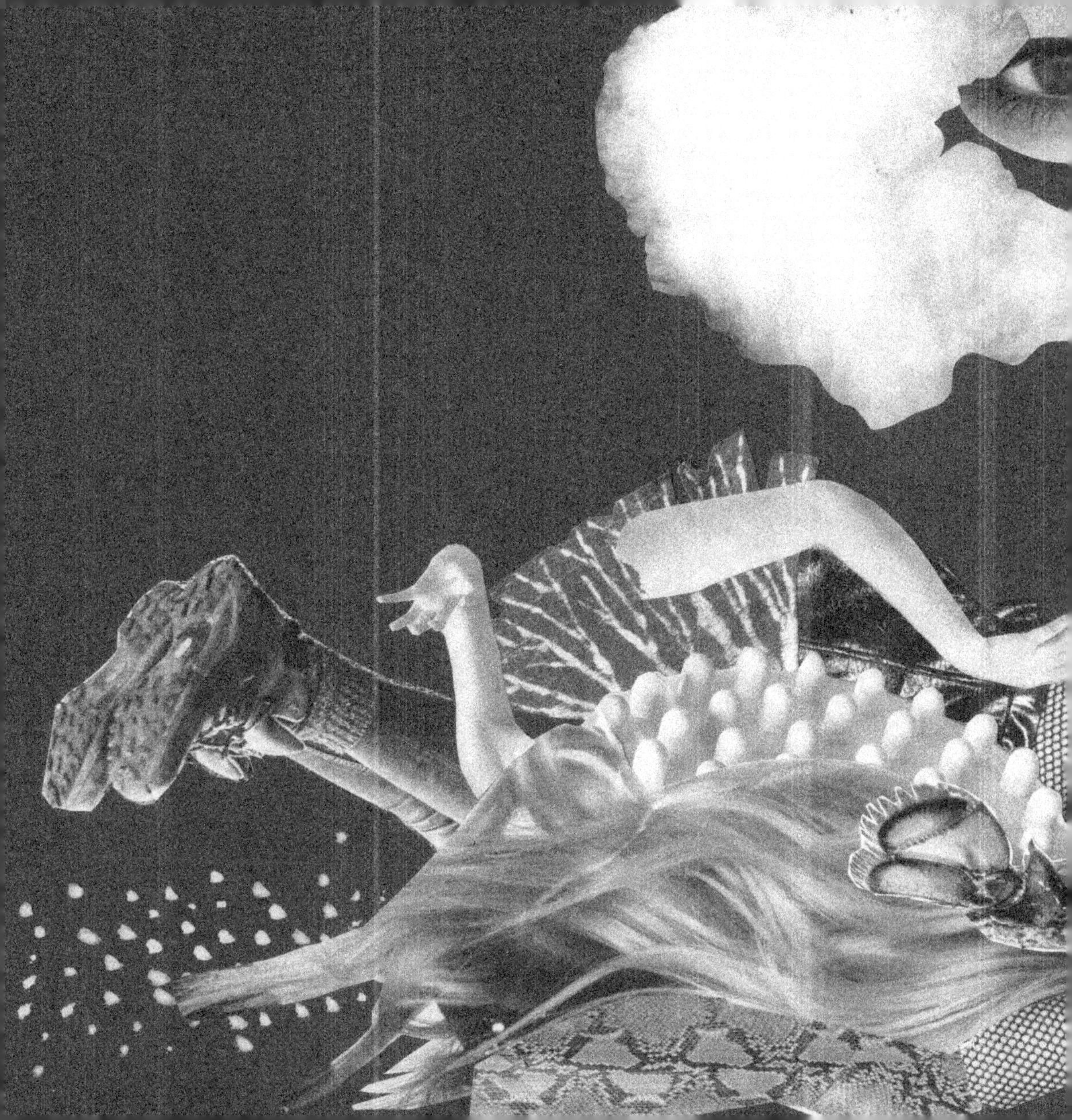

Being human

Rosa Parks, who said no to Jim Crow
by refusing to give up her seat on a bus
is Mother
of the American Civil Rights Movement

Marina Abramovich, who walked the Great Wall
of China to break up with her lover
is Grandmother
of Performance Art

Germaine Greer, 2nd wave feminist
who spars with her pen
her tongue
her wit

Helen Keller
Lee Lin Chin
Cassandra, Threasa, Seana, Indigo
Lyndall, Joanna, Simmo & Bron

Wild wicked wonder women
these are my heroes
Fearless teachers and leaders
none of them breeders

But this is not a poem
in defence of childless women
                    Nu-uh,
This is an ode to being human
7.6 billion humans, actually
and, like sea levels, still rising

To breed or not to breed

Is that the question
on which this planet depends?
And while you ponder that
we childless women and men
are not to be pitied
I am no barren womb
I am childless by

deliberate

          difficult

choice

And yet, that old maternal myth
shows up in every religion
from Hindu goddess to Catholic virgin

I don't know about you
but the whole worship-a-virgin thing
didn't impregnate me
with a wild desire for parenting

Parking women's power in pregnancy
                    Damn! that's bad poetry!

See, mothers are more than mothers
and we are all fertile ground
like the time my right tit gave birth

to twelve gold nipples

I sat on my golden throne

nursing twelve gold babies

like Cassandra, Threasa, Seana, Indigo

Lyndall, Joanna, Simmo & Bron

      who create and fight with vigour

      who have so much life they do not lack

      will not surrender

      and in this way

      they become

HUMAN

Liar

sometimes   the poem you want to write is a lie   sometimes
  to lie is to live is to need is to write is to poem is to lie
          sometimes
  on slow spring mornings you don't know
which suffering you want to lie down with
like a damaged dog
      so the despair chooses you
            sometimes
      the poem wants to lie
  and the lie has been written as truth
      like we are all born equal
          like world peace is possible
like the left is righter than the right is righter than the left
            these fine fine lies
              these failed stories

sometimes
      the story you want to write won't arrive
          no matter how hard you try

                         no matter how many words you run into
          you
                    just
                         run
                              out
                                   of ....
so   you lie
         and in the lie you might find something else is alive

                         a surprise that's kind of nice and lyrical
     like
         there's a blizzard of sad stars imploding underneath my skin
when what's really going on is
     this unfamiliar chaos of wrinkle and sag and –

                                        unreliable memory

     these solid Double Ds have slipped into Es
          like   two soft fists in the fight against time
     this sudden hot flash of feeling hopelessly redundant

irrelevant

invisible

is that a lie?

am I a liar?

are you?

is it okay to lie?

to pick up words like a hot solar wind

then chuck them like pieces of space junk

into crazy patterns

and each crazy is a poem you will propagate

and each pattern is a point of no return

because you lied?

even when the lie opens up your mind to something bigger

like

a Giant Celestial Phantom who says:

Hey, Caroline –
You wanna speak your smooth talking lies into this microphone?

Go ahead.

Some of my best friends are liars.

And I'm totes good with that.

Bella's wedding

there were lots of people at the
wedding they smelt nice she
told them all how nice they smelt her
dad said confetti is coloured snow that doesn't melt her
mum got bits of confetti stuck in her
long hair her mum has short hair now she
ran and spilt Coke on her orange dress same as her
sister they're not twins her
brother is very small he

wore a green shirt with coconut buttons he

got the first piece of cake her

shoes got ruined in the mud she

jumped in with the boys until a stone hit her

nose and mum sat with her

on a bench next to the quiet lake she

picked snow out of mum's hair and ate it her

mouth and fingers turned rainbow she

fell asleep like that her dad took a photo she

cried when she saw it

half her face

was

cut

off

love

one more time
one more time, Fiona
and I will leave you
you got it?
HAVE YOU GOT IT?
one more time
and i will leave you
for fucking good

Cultural submissions

I'm calling in to see someone in a world grown-ups know nothing about, sitting snug on their living room couches. The thing about that is this – I think it doesn't matter, Mary thinks I'm lost in the wrong kitchen, or to put it another way, I'm hungry all through to the bedroom, you know how windy it gets in Perth, it really hollows you out.

I listen all the way to Melbourne – a new thing for me – in the front
seat with Mary's half-brother. Mary likes me and the radio, eats
sausage meat in the mirror after peeling back the flaky pastry but
that's become irrelevant. I bark about a blank page, four weeks of
drinking in Fitzroy, swerving –

There is no rent to pay for a squat with ocean liners painted on the
walls overlooking a car park. The now-defunct tram conductor swaps
places with the driver, neither saying where they are racing us to or
how far there is to go or what is needed to make sense of Henna Wash
shampoo promising a lasting colour, Superman with a fist down
his pants – his blue and red style really leaping out – a handful of
teenagers breaking the law in summer itself, drive-through coffee,
'The Lord is Merciful' headlines.

Me and Mary find a corner stool, listen to Chris Wilson blow the big
picture, stare at copper water pipes, over-watch blue sky, drink at
the wheel. I don't know what I'm s'posed to do with any of this. Mary
answers like an anthropologist who sounds like a mirage – 'Like any
primitive culture, we have our ceremonies. Staring out of windows,
eating pies with tomato sauce, drawing a pint of bitter from the
wrong side of the bar. The messages, the stories, like mouth organs or
kangaroos, you just submit as often as you wish.'

this little poem

will disappoint you
like a seafood laksa
with only one prawn

this little poem
will surprise you
like walking in on Peter Dutton
masturbating
and when you come back
three years later
he is still masturbating

this little poem
wears steam punk mascara
a boiler suit stolen from MONA
a bling bling belt and
Penny Wong as her poster girl

she is trying to be a proper poem

but her papers (like her parents) were lost at sea

or torched by a parliament of pricks

or drowned in a bloat of oil and blood

and unbelievable ego

and who listened when she reported

the corruption of the administration?

so it looks like they'll get away with it

this little poem

weighs a black ton of sorrow

like a political storm fast approaching

so it looks like

we're in for a rough night

this little poem

travelled by little boat

to the Atlas Mountains

to listen to the history

of other little poems

it seemed like the right place to be

until it wasn't

but she can't stop searching

and she won't stop gathering together

all the little threads of all the little poems

rolling them between her fingers

until they become the greasy rag

spilling into your drink

and this little poem won't stop talking

she is the reason

you will go to the bar

for your third drinks special

or go outside to see

if another

better poem

is coming

like a small red boat

prodding a vast green sea in a hurricane

this little poem

draws on hope

for survival

like laughter carried by wind
over an anxious land
this little poem lands
like the promises politicians
make all the time
on podiums and pavements
on billboards and in bars
that when you spin around suddenly
to face them head on –

they are gone.

Ollie's blood roses

I get home in the early hours of the morning with a bunch of blood roses. Mum sits in the dark on the verandah, fan in one hand, fag in the other. 'I thought you were staying at Steph's,' she says.

'Change of plan,' I say, flopping into the old blue armchair.

'Wanna talk about it?'

'Nope.' Steph and me argue all the time and I never want to talk about it.

'I don't know what you see in that girl. Where d'you get those roses?' she says, crushing her fag out in the Vegemite jar.

'Ollie said they're for you.' I set them down on the corner of the crate between us.

'He's a sweetheart. I'll go thank him tomorrow. Lock up when you're done.'

She takes the roses inside but leaves the packet of Alpines open on the crate. The flywire slams behind her and I'm left listening to the crickets on my own. After arguing with Steph I usually nick a couple of Mum's beers, smoke her fags, go to bed and try to forget about it. But tonight is different. It's like Ollie said, those blood roses are making me want to spill my guts. So I talk to the crickets, smoke curling out of my mouth.

It started when Steph and me went out for one of our midnight walks down to Cisco's to find some action. Heat's oozing out the pavement. Our clothes are sticking to us. Steph starts complaining about her thighs getting sore from rubbing together. She's wearing a skirt, which I told her was a bad idea, but it's new and floral and she wants to try it out. I find an old shopping trolley and Steph flashes her gash getting into the thing. The wonky wheel makes it hard going so I'm wheezing like an old dog by the time we get to Cisco's. None of the crew is there. Midnight is probably a bit early. We go into the deli anyway, to cool down and wait. A tall, topless kid holds the door open for us before he heads out. His jeans are pushed down below his hips, a dark line of hair snaking up his belly. The silver sleepers in both nipples bounce when his pecs twitch.

'Evenin', Miss,' he says.

I could hardly hear him over the sound of the electronic buzzer. Steph wiggles her fingers hello, and I go to do the same, cool and casual, but my hand has a mind of its own and somehow manages to brush his groin, just the teeniest touch. Nipple Boy winks at me. The only guys who ever wink at me are drunks and weirdos, so I'm completely thrown. The door slams shut before I have time to say anything and I watch Nipple Boy ride off on a pushbike that's stupidly small for him. I want to run down the road after him.

'Did you ever hear about that woman on Mawson Parade who grew tomatoes?' says Steph, adjusting her skirt before sitting down.

'Nope, I never did.'

'Yeah ya did,' she insists. 'Just past O'Kane's place. That big old house with the rusty gate and no fence. Grass overgrown. Mad old woman.'

'Oh yeah, I know the place.' I wish she would shut up so I could concentrate on what I'm going to do about Nipple Boy. I look out the window for him and catch a flash of his bare back sailing under a streetlight. He looks like some wide-winged meaty angel about to take off.

'That old woman killed her kids,' says Steph.

'Yeah, right.'

'Two of them.' Her silver charm bracelet jangles as she holds up two fingers like I don't know what two is. 'There's a light goes on every night, back of the house.'

'So?' I say.

She leans into me like it's a big secret. 'So no-one lives there. No-one's lived there for years.'

'Squatters.'

'They say it's haunted.'

'Who the hell are *they*?'

'Everyone.' She rubs the heart charm on her bracelet. 'Anyhoo, that woman won awards for her tomatoes.'

Cisco's sign flashes neon red in the window. The traffic lights change on the corner and a dude in black runs the red light on his Harley, hair streaming like a soft devil's tail. Steph follows my look to where Nipple Boy is doing dusty doughnuts on his weeny bike, showing off.

'Nice nipple rings on that one,' she says.

'I accidentally touched his cock when we came in.'

Steph hoots with laughter, hand over her mouth.

'I'm going for it,' I say. 'Once I cool down a bit, I'm going over to talk to him, definitely.' You have to spell things out for Steph when it comes to blokes. If you've got your eye on someone, let her know, or she'll jump in ahead of you. I'm imagining sweaty sex with Nipple Boy, a long slow job like I saw three nights ago when I was snooping around the back of that house on Mawson Parade, the one Steph says is haunted. I saw bodies in the moonlight through the broken glass. I know the place isn't haunted. I'm getting horny as hell thinking about skin and cock and Nipple Boy while Steph carries on with her tomato talk.

'Have to keep soil in the root zone moist. Moisture is very important.'

I never grew a tomato in my life. I buy them in tins, all ready for tipping into the pot. Steph can't get over it. She's learnt from her dad some old Italian way of growing and bottling. I have to admit it, Steph is a really great tomato grower. The best. I've never done anything that good in my life. But I don't want to hear her tomato talk tonight. I don't want to hear her talking like she's in some special club, like she's got one up on me, like growing tomatoes is going to change the world. Feeling mean, I go to the fridge to get drinks. Steph's voice goes up a notch as I move across the lino tiles.

'Stalk borers and stink bugs, they suck the juices!' she squeals.

I want to crawl into Cisco's fridge, somewhere cool and quiet, so I can figure out what I'm going to say to Nipple Boy.

'Jumping bugs make the plants look like they've been shot full of holes,' Steph squeaks, her voice so high it sounds like she's putting it on.

'Pension day tomorrow?' asks Ollie when I dump a handful of shrapnel on the counter to pay for the drinks. Ollie's been working the graveyard shift at Cisco's for years. It's his second job. He sends money home to India. His whole family lives there. He's always friendly, always smiling. On the counter there's a single bunch of red roses in a bucket. They look fresh and neat, just like Ollie.

'Just make it one. Lemonade is on the house.' He pushes most of the shrapnel back across the counter.

'I'm not a charity case,' I say.

'Charity begins at home,' says Ollie.

'Thanks,' I say, and swallow the lump in my throat.

Back at the table Steph starts bragging about how much her tomatoes have grown, says the biggest one grew a whole inch to five inches. Overnight. 'A tomato with a diameter of eleven centimetres,' she says, doing the conversion for me, like I can't figure it out for myself. 'Can you believe it?'

I can hardly believe it. But I know Steph wouldn't lie to me about that. She pops open her tomato juice, takes a sip, licks her top lip, smooths back her dark curls and runs a finger under her eyes to keep the melting mascara in check. All in one fluid movement.

'Eleven centimetres is not really very big.'

'Says you, who can't even grow a cactus,' she bites back.

'What's the world record for the biggest tomato?'

'I'm not doing it for any records. I'm doing it to keep tradition alive,' she says.

That really gets to me. I mean, what's wrong with admitting to your best friend that you want to grow the world's biggest tomato?

'You wanna be in the *Guinness Book of Records*,' I say, like it's the dumbest thing in the world to want.

'Cactus killer,' she says and folds her arms.

'That's right, Steph. I can kill a cactus no worries. I can do the impossible. I'm a fucking superhero.' I crack open my lemonade and drink until the gas hurts my throat.

Nipple Boy is stopped in the vacant block opposite Cisco's, legs straddling that baby bike. All I want is for him to dink me on the back of his deadly-treadly, off to that old house on Mawson Parade and get sweaty with him on a dirty mattress. I stand up.

'Why are you all shitty?' says Steph. '*You're* the one who started it. Now you're walking out on me?'

It was true. But something didn't fit. I remembered the last time we argued. Steph bought me a cactus as a sorry present. A succulent, she called it.

'Succulents don't need much water. They thrive on neglect.' That's exactly what she said. And then it slips into place. Steph expected that cactus to die. She was just waiting for me to kill it so she could laugh and tell me how useless I was, which is pretty much the way it went.

'Why did you buy me that cactus, Steph?' I'm surprised at how loud my voice is.

I know Ollie is listening. Steph stares at me for a second, then bursts out laughing and tosses her hair just as Cisco's buzzer cuts in.

'Hello, ladies,' says Nipple Boy, wiggling his hips a little, the thick warm night coming in with him.

I'm not ready. I trip on the thin metal leg of the table and knock over my lemonade. But it's just a little spill. So I straighten the can, plaster on a smile, cross my fingers behind my back, and am about to say something witty when Nipple Boy cruises past me like I'm not there. Steph crosses her legs and fiddles with the hem of her skirt. Ollie calls me over.

'What?' I yell, not moving.

Steph flashes me a look as if to say *what are you going to do about it?* Nipple Boy is smiling at Steph like he just won the lottery. Ollie calls me again. I can't be rude to Ollie. He's like the friendliest guy in the world, so I go to the counter.

'What?' I say, trying to be patient.

'I have something for you.'

'Can't it wait?'

'No. Come out back. Now.'

I follow him into the kitchen. He opens the cool room door.

'In there.' He signals for me to go in. When I'm in the cool room he shuts the door quickly and locks it from the outside. I bang on the metal door. I swear at him to let me out. 'You sit there and cool down,' he shouts. Not in a mean way. Just so I can hear him through the thick steel.

Twenty minutes later he lets me out. Steph and Nipple Boy have gone.

'Thanks a lot, Ollie.' I sulk, wanting to take my bad mood out on someone. But he isn't having it.

'If she was your friend she would have stayed,' he says. 'She would have waited and said no to that boy. If she was a true friend.'

'Steph just gets carried away when it comes to blokes. She's alright.' But I'm feeling down about the whole thing.

'Take these.' Ollie offers me roses from the bucket. 'Blood roses. You go home. You give them to Mum. You tell her what happened. You listen to what she says about your friend.'

'Mum and I don't talk about this stuff, Ollie.'

'These are special flowers.' He presses them gently into my hands. 'You give Mum the roses. And you talk. She will listen. Then, things will be different.'

Now I'm sitting on Mum's bed after waking her up, smelling those sweet roses in a coffee jar on the bedside table. Outside, the crickets are still chirruping and the sky is so black and starless it feels like the whole world could be swallowed up in its dark mouth. Mum is telling me it's alright to cry, rubbing my back until I'm ready to talk. And when I do, I'll tell her about Steph and her tomatoes, the cactus and Ollie's blood roses. I will let her listen to everything.

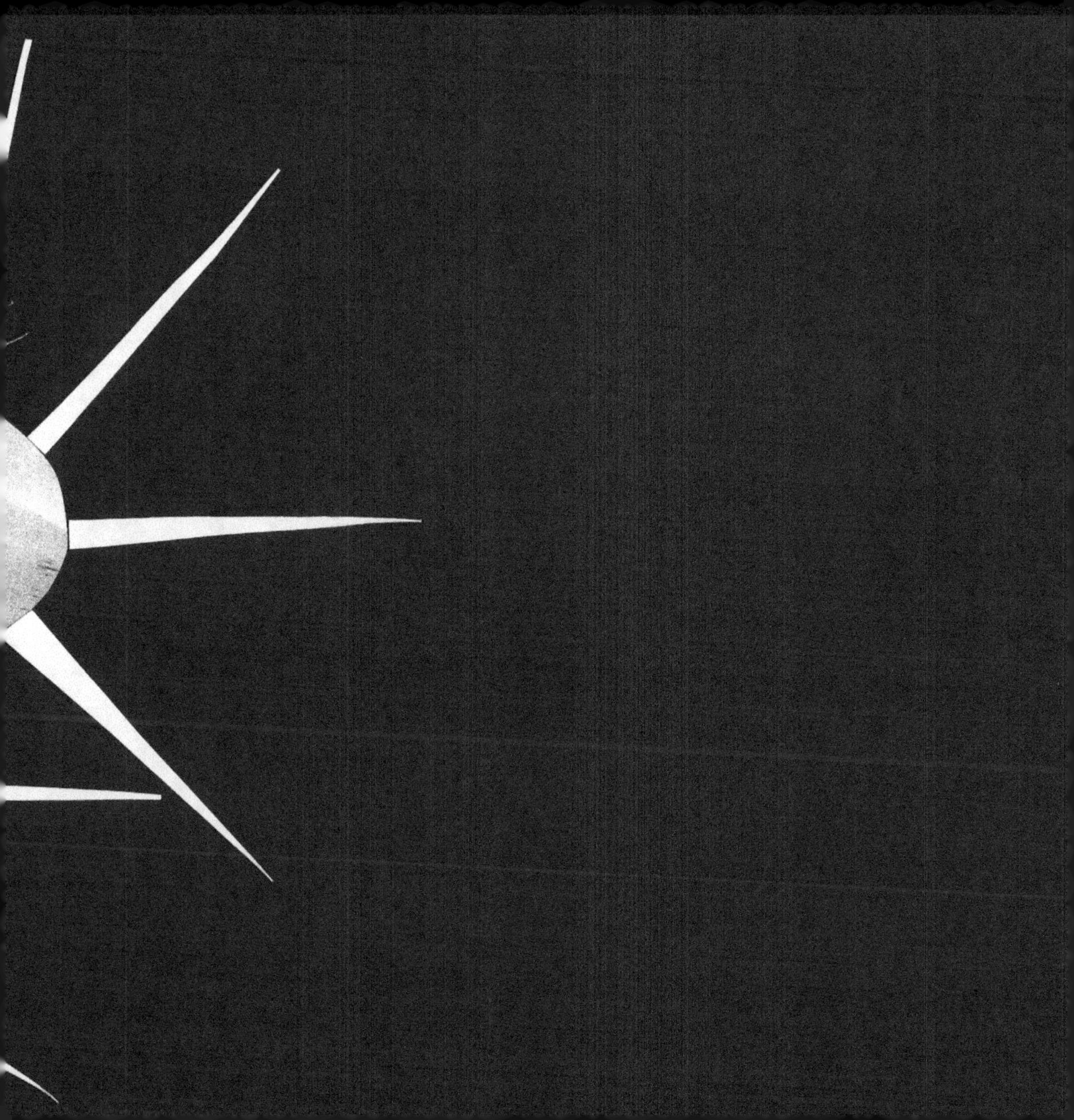

Just for Jesus

In November Tim gave me a bible. It was small in my hands. A King James Bible covered in faded black cloth, the spine brittle, pages edged in pink. They might have been red once.

'I know you like old things,' he said.

There were eighteen candles on the cake in the hotel room. I blew them out in one hectic breath then Tim unzipped me. I got my first bible when I was thirteen, when Mum decided the public school system wasn't good enough for me so she saved her pennies and packed me off to Our Lady of the Sacred Heart. At first I thought Jesus was like Elvis, pretty and famous, and that God had written all those hymns we sang in church just for Jesus.

'How cool to have a father who writes songs for you,' I said.

'Don't worry about all that mumbo jumbo stuff, just get on with your studies,' Mum said.

In December Tim took me out in his boat. The sky was vivid with silvery clouds. The green sea foamed and gurgled. We'd been drinking red wine the night before and I vomited pink over the side of the boat. Lying on the narrow bed below deck, I looked up to see a double rainbow through the cabin window. Tim said I was a good luck charm. He wrapped a big snapper in newspaper for me. I didn't know how I was going to explain the fish to Mum, so I threw it away. Tim and his wife went to New Zealand for Christmas.

In January Tim caught me sniffing the crotch of his pants in the hotel room. He always wore proper pants, never jeans.

'My wife does my washing,' he said, snatching them out from under my nose.

I thought his pants smelt like they'd started their life before I had, but I didn't mention it. He was already super upset because after I went down on him I told him I found a grey pube.

In February I started uni and Tim took me out fishing again. He stood behind me and showed me how to steer the boat. I loved feeling his heat against my back. He told me he and his wife were breaking up, that she nagged him about everything, that she didn't want him to have any fun. Even the boat – she reckoned – was a total waste of money.

'I think it's a nice boat,' I said.

'Oh, Princess,' he said, holding my face in his hands. 'You're the one who understands me. I've booked us a holiday in Bali next month, just the two of us.'

I told Mum I was going to visit a friend.

In March Tim said his wife had arranged – at the last minute – for the two of them to go on a cruise.

'I'm so sorry, Princess,' he said. 'But don't worry, Bali is not cancelled, just postponed.'

'What happened to going to visit that friend?' Mum asked.

I told her my friend had died.

In April our lease wasn't renewed so Mum and I had to move again. Tim called to tell me he and his wife were going to Fiji – at the last minute. Mum said the whole block of flats could hear me the way I was carrying on like a pork chop.

'Did he tell you his wife's a bitch?' she said. 'Did he tell you she doesn't understand him? That he's going to leave her?'

I threw my phone at her. It didn't break but it gouged a massive hole in the wall. The real estate agent took money out of our bond to fix it.

In May, on her way to the new flat, Mum got hit by a car. She was in intensive care with a smashed hip, her head split open like a coconut, her face bruised the colour of the King James Bible. She didn't speak. The doctor said it was shock, that she'd come around in her own good time. A week later the swelling had gone down but she still hadn't said anything. While I was packing up my room, I found the bible under my bed. I took it with me to the university church where I sat in the back pew feeling sad and cold. Its pages were as fragile as breath. I didn't read, just carefully turned the pages hoping I would absorb something holy or that Jesus would forgive me, even though I knew that was about as likely as Mum doing the same. I lit a candle for her, then one for me, and stared into the flickety flames as the stained glass windows darkened above me. I thought about how church windows are always so far away, way above the people

Yesterday, Tim came to the flat. He paced the kitchen wearing jeans and the blue Fijian shirt his wife had bought him. I told him I'd been singing hymns to Mum in hospital and the first thing she said was, 'Will you stop that mumbo jumbo. Don't you know any Elvis?'

Tim didn't laugh. He said Elvis was a mama's boy with a serious eating disorder and a God complex. I sprayed him with lemon-scented Pine-O-Cleen. He offered me a week's rent. I told him I'd already quit uni and got a job. He looked into the empty coffee cup and asked if I'd be okay.

I said, 'What about that holiday, mate?'

He told me he and his wife had turned a corner.

After he'd gone I sat on the red lino in the kitchen with my second-hand bible. At the end of the Book of Revelations someone had drawn a naked man with an oversized cock spurting pink ink across the page. I wrote 'Tim' under the picture. Then I ripped the page out and ate it. It tasted dry and dirty, like an old man's skin.

One blue eye

The dog at the BP in Fitzroy Crossing had one blue eye, a torn ear and a mind opened by the wound in the top of her head. Even Dave looked twice. And it takes a lot for Dave to react. On the dry grass verge behind the dog, a blue heeler waited, uncertain of the outcome of the fight. Had he been won or not? And if so, why was she stalling? Balls twitching, lipstick out, he sniffed the air for a clue. The dog didn't move.

A slow parade of muddy four-wheel drives and campervans steered clear of her. Grown-ups and children rubber-necked to gawp at the dried-blood-dress, the one blue eye, the ten-mile stare, the meaty crown. She wasn't moving. 'Tough bitch,' said Dave. 'You wanna coffee?' He parked away from the dog, giving her a wide berth on his trek to the roadhouse, just like everyone else. Her circle of stillness was sacred. Her place had teeth. She wasn't about to lick her wounds in public.

Cooked bones

Wednesday

At 3:07am, for the fourth consecutive morning, Frank Murphy wakes to a barking dog. His wife, Pam, snores. He shifts about in the bed until she stirs.

'You're snoring.'

She turns her back to him.

'Bloody dog. I'll kill it.'

'Get the earplugs,' Pam mumbles in the dark.

'I'm going to see,' Frank says, and gets out of bed.

He switches on the kitchen light then unlocks the front door. He hears the toilet flush while he stands outside in the dark, unsure of what to do next.

Pam opens the flywire door. 'What are you going to do?'

'I'm going to shut that dog up,' he says.

Pam watches him stride down the driveway in his Superman boxer shorts. It's a hot night so he hasn't bothered to put on a shirt. His belly hangs white and hairy over his shorts. Pam considers going back to bed but she stays standing in the doorway. Frank gets as far as the front gate then stops, hands on hips.

'Shut up!' he yells at the dog across the road. 'Shut up! Shut up! Shut up!'

Pam laughs to herself. She thinks her husband looks like an overweight superhero who's forgotten he lost his power a long time ago. But the dog has stopped barking. It's a brown staffy, well lit in the amber streetlight, standing still, tail raised. It watches Frank through a hole in the black hessian that lines the cyclone fencing. Frank stands his ground and glares at the dog. Pam giggles. As a warning to the dog, Frank wags a finger and yells again before heading inside. But as soon as his back is turned the dog begins to bark. Frank stomps barefoot across the road to where the dog is going crazy, picks up a good-sized rock and throws it. Even though he's at close range, his aim is bad and the rock hits the letterbox. Frank picks up another rock and throws that too. Then another, and another. The dog yelps. The barking stops briefly. When it starts again, the staffy sounds like it wants to tear Frank apart.

Pam feels pricks of heat on her chest and arms as she dashes across the road to her husband. The dog is lunging at Frank, its front paws hitting the fence, streaks of silver saliva flying in the darkness. Pam is glad of the fence between them. Frank grabs the cyclone fencing, rattling it with both hands while he shouts at the dog. The dog continues to lunge, snapping at Frank's hands. Pam becomes uneasy when her husband begins growling and snarling at the dog.

'Stop acting like an idiot,' she says.

But Frank keeps on growling, hands firmly fastened to the fence.

Pam grips his shoulders. She is trying to drag him away when a sudden pain in Frank's right hand causes him to jerk the arm back, and as he does he hits Pam in the face.

'Bloody thing bit me!'

'Come away,' Pam whispers, holding her cheek. 'Frankie, come away.'

Inside, Frank lumbers to the bathroom. In the glare of the mirror he sees the ragged tear across three of his fingers and the blood on his wife's cheek. He leans over the bathroom sink, struggling for breath, sweat dribbling from his chin, blood dripping from his fingers. It feels like something has been drained out of him. He can still hear the dog barking.

Pam cleans the blood off her face then bandages his hand. 'You'll need a tetanus shot,' she says.

'How's your face?'

'I'll live.'

'It was an accident.' He clenches his teeth.

'I know. Come to bed.'

There's a red mark on her cheek and dark bags under her eyes. I'm sorry, he thinks, but the words don't come out of his mouth.

'That's enough excitement for one night, Superman.' She yawns.

'I'm not tired,' he says. 'I'm going to watch a bit of TV.'

He is tired but the incident with the dog has unnerved him. After smoking a cigarette, he phones the police. The policewoman says she can't do anything. Frank insists she take his details. She does, then suggests he contact the council in the morning. He thanks her very much and says he will most certainly be doing that.

Pam is snoring by the time he gets to bed. He sits down on the single bed in the spare room and stuffs fluoro orange earplugs into his ears. He can still hear the dog barking. It barks on and off for three hours. The sky has changed from heavy black to a milky blue when Frank finally falls asleep. He dreams he is being chased through the house by a noisy shadow. He can't tell if it's a dog or something bigger. The alarm goes off at seven. He is at work by eight.

'Nuisance barking. We get it a lot,' says Susan, the girl at the council. She explains the procedure to him over the phone: 'Keep a diary for two weeks. Whenever the dog barks, write it down. Include everything – when it started, how long it barked for, when it stopped. It doesn't matter what time, day or night, write it all down.'

'I work during the day. I don't know if it barks then,' Frank says.

'Just do what you can. Send it through to me and I'll contact the owner.'

'Is that it?'

'Any action we take will depend on whether the owner gets the dog to stop,' says Susan.

'I have to wait two weeks?'

'That's usual,' she says.

'Can't you send someone around today?'

'That's not usual.'

'I haven't slept for weeks. That's not usual either.'

'Don't get mad, Mr Murphy. That's not helpful.'

'I'm not mad, Susan,' he says, keeping his voice calm. 'I may sound mad but I'm just sleep deprived. On account of the dog. You understand.'

'Oh, I understand.'

'Anyway, I don't get mad, I get even,' Frank says, as a joke.

There is a pause on the other end of the phone.

'I'm not serious, Susan.'

'You could write them an anonymous letter, Mr Murphy. Drop it in their letterbox. If you want.'

'You mean threaten them?' He is surprised Susan is telling him this.

'We, at the council, do not condone violence against animals, Mr Murphy. It's against policy. It's my duty to let you know that.'

'That's what I thought—'

'Just let them know their dog is causing a disturbance. Most people are pretty good about fixing it.'

'Okay—' Frank says.

'But no threats.'

'No threats,' says Frank.

'Thank you, Mr Murphy. Is there anything else we can help you with today?'

At lunchtime Frank drives out to the cliffs to eat his ham, cheese and pickle sandwiches. He watches boats gently prod the green sea. There is a thin line of cloud on the horizon. He takes out his work diary. In the 'Extra Comments' section at the bottom of the page he writes 'Dog barked this morning 3:07 – 6:15 am.' He writes the same for Tuesday,

Monday and Sunday then closes the diary. He opens it again and carefully rips a page out of the back of the book. In tidy capital letters he prints a note to the dog owner. He signs it 'Sick and Tired Neighbour'.

By the time he gets home that evening his hand aches. So do his eyes. He takes three Panadol, washing them down with dry cider.

'You should go to the doctor,' says Pam, as she serves them up lamb shank stew.

'Maybe.'

'Before that hand starts festering.' She plonks his meal on the table. 'You want to watch *Burke's Backyard*?'

They sit on separate armchairs in the lounge room. Frank picks at his dinner. The shanks are tough. A vet describes to Don Burke what can happen to the insides of a dog when you feed it cooked bones.

'The bones splinter and damage the dog's mouth, throat and insides. They can cause serious injury or even death,' says the vet.

Images of dogs drooling blood end any hope Frank has of finishing his dinner. He takes the half-eaten shanks into the kitchen, scrapes them into the bin and opens his work diary.

'Could you drop this into their letterbox?' he says, handing Pam the note. A purple bruise has formed on her cheek.

She takes it and reads it. 'The dog doesn't keep me awake,' she says, handing it back to him.

'It will look less suspicious if you do it,' he says.

'Frankie, go talk to them. Why are you bothering with a letter? It puts people off.'

'You're my wife. Surely it's not too much to ask.'

She snatches the letter from him. Frank stands at the lounge room window watching her stride cross the road. He stands at the window long after Pam returns, long after she finishes her bath and is ready for bed. He has a smoke and goes to the kitchen now and then for a fresh bottle of cider. He watches the hole in the black hessian that lines the cyclone fencing but he doesn't see or hear the dog.

Thursday

Frank wakes at 3:07 am. He shakes his wife roughly.

'You're snoring.'

'Frank! Are you going to write me a letter?' She hits him with her pillow then storms out of the room, taking the pillow with her.

The toilet flushes. The light goes on in the spare room. Frank lies in the dark, cupping the throbbing, bitten hand to his chest. The light goes off in the spare room. He gets up. He takes three Panadol. The dog isn't barking.

'Come back to bed,' he says to the closed door.

Susan calls Frank at work.

'I was able to do a house call this morning, Mr Murphy. I talked to the owners.'

Frank's surprise at her efficiency stops him from saying anything.

'You wrote a letter.'

'Uh-huh,' says Frank.

'Tyson's owners—'

'Tyson?' he asks.

'The dog's name is Tyson, Mr Murphy. His owners have made a complaint against you.'

'For writing a letter?'

'Did you injure Tyson, Mr Murphy?'

'Injure?'

'Tyson sustained damage near an eye socket. Three stitches were required.'

Frank swallows.

'I said no threats Mr Murphy.'

'There were no threats.'

'The owners are very upset. And vets aren't cheap.'

Frank waits to be asked to cough up.

'Do you have a dog, Mr Murphy?'

'No.'

'I see.'

Frank hears Susan typing. 'Look, Susan. That dog. Tyson. He barks every night. I'm sure there are other people—'

'You're the only one who's made a complaint, Mr Murphy.'

He hears more typing. 'I've started a diary,' he says, and clears his throat.

The typing stops. Susan sighs. 'We, at council, do not condone violence against animals, Mr Murphy. You should know that.'

'I would never deliberately harm a dog.'

'So you're saying it wasn't you?'

'It wasn't me.'

In the doctor's room Frank's hand pulses with pain. He holds it gingerly while telling Dr Marone about the barking dog and lack of sleep. The doctor cleans and re-bandages Frank's injured hand.

'It's rare to get fifty-six year old men in here, Mr Murphy. How about we run some tests while we've got you?'

'Do I have to?'

'It can't hurt,' says the doctor. 'What breed of dog was it?'

'My wife says it's a staffy. I don't know much about dogs.'

'Did you know that recent studies show dogs can smell cancer in humans?'

Frank's stomach lurches. 'Are you saying I've got cancer?'

'Not at all. Um … how many cigarettes a day do you smoke?'

Because he is ashamed, Frank lies about the smokes, the cider, the lack of exercise. But he can't fudge his blood pressure and weight. Dr Marone's face is impassive as he listens to Frank's chest through the stethoscope.

'Well, Mr Murphy, you have high blood pressure, you're overweight, and no amount of smoking is good for you. Have you tried patches?'

'I've tried everything, mate.'

The doctor smiles. 'We might have to work on that. In the meantime, I'd like to take some blood and send you for X-rays.'

Frank hears his heart thumping in protest. 'What for?'

'The blood is for cholesterol, prostate and blood sugar checks. The X-rays are for your lungs. You can put your shirt back on.'

Blood drains from Frank's face. His mouth goes dry. He feels like he's going to pass out. The doctor looks up from where he's scribbling.

'Are you alright Mr Murphy?' He puts a hand softly on the older man's leg. 'Just lie down for a minute.'

Frank does as he's told. When he closes his eyes he sees dogs vomiting blood and his wife's bruised cheek.

'I'm guessing it's been a while since you've seen a doctor?'

Frank nods.

'You'll need to thank that dog then. I'm not trying to scare you, Mr Murphy, but we can't be too careful at your age. You might want to seriously consider making some lifestyle changes.'

Frank cringes at the word. As far as he's concerned, *lifestyle* is something only the rich can afford.

'Walking is an easy option and doesn't cost anything,' says the doctor. 'You could walk in the mornings when that dog wakes you. You might find it helps you sleep—'

'Putting that bloody dog down is the only thing that'll help me sleep!' Frank's voice sounds very loud in the small room.

The doctor turns to face his patient and tells him to sit up. Frank does as he's told.

'I put it to you, Mr Murphy, that the reason you're not sleeping is your compromised health, not the barking dog.' Dr Marone speaks as gently as he can.

The house is in darkness when Frank gets home. He looks for a note from his wife but there isn't one. He opens a can of bourbon and coke then lights a cigarette. When he's finished he throws the can and butt in the bin on top of the half-eaten shanks. He takes the referral papers out of his pocket, smooths them out and looks at his name written in the doctor's small handwriting: Frank Murphy. 56-year-old male. He opens the bin, fishes out a couple of shanks and puts them on the kitchen bench next to the papers. He opens another can, takes a gulp, then considers the shanks. He pictures the mongrel dog his wife bought the kids when they were small, a silly mutt that didn't know its arse from its elbow. It was eight years old when it died. Bloody fool dog didn't get out of the way when Frank reversed the car one night. The scream it made was terrible. The dog's pelvis was broken. It had to be put down. Pam and the kids were heartbroken, cried for days. Frank does the maths and realises he's the same age in human years as the mongrel dog was when it died.

He goes to the bathroom, takes off his shirt, and looks at himself in the mirror, front-on and from the side.

'Bought and paid for,' he says to the reflection, slapping his hard belly. He puts his shirt back on. He grabs the shanks from the kitchen bench and heads across the road. When he gets to the hole in the hessian he cocks his head, listens for the dog. He can't hear anything.

'Tyson,' he says in a low voice. 'Tyson.'

An inside light shines at the far end of the house.

'Tyson,' he says again. 'C'mon, you mutt.' He taps the shanks against the fence so it rattles. 'C'mon, boy.'

There are voices and a familiar laugh at the front of the house. The outside light goes on and the back door opens. Tyson shoots out across the lawn and pisses against a tree next to overgrown bushes in the corner of the yard.

'Tyson,' Frank calls quietly. 'Tyson, come here, boy.'

When the dog races over, Frank throws the shanks so they land with a thud in the yard. Tyson pounces. He tries to fit both shanks in his mouth at the same time.

'Stupid mutt'. Frank snickers.

'Frank?' says Pam, rounding the corner. 'Were you on your way over?'

Frank starts, turning quickly to face his wife on the pavement, his back against the fence, arms spread wide trying to hide the evidence of dog and bones. His shirt is sticking to his back, his throat is dry.

'You needn't bother. I've just sorted things out,' she says. 'They know it was you. I told them you'd pay the vet's bill. They're nice people, very upset.'

'I went to the doctor,' says Frank.

There is a sharp crack in the darkness. Pam gets closer to the fence, pushes Frank aside and peers through the hole in the hessian. Tyson has one of the shanks between his front paws like it's a lollipop, cracking it open with his powerful back teeth to get at the marrow.

'Frank,' she says. 'Are they *our* bones?'

The panic Frank felt in the doctor's surgery returns. 'The doctor says I'm sick, Pam.'

She stares at him. Her voice is steady, accusing. 'You fed the dog cooked bones?' Without waiting for an answer, she turns on her heels and hurries away from him back the way she came.

'Wait, Pam! I'm sick!'

Distracted by the din, Tyson stops chomping on his bone and watches the shouting man.

'The doctor says I've got cancer. Pammy! I'm sick! *I'm sick!*'

Stars

for Stompy

You didn't laugh when you told me you had penile cancer

I did

I'm not proud

I think it was shock

I remember the time we pissed ourselves over words like

important and impotent

eunuch and unique

I remember a woman laughing in a dream,

she said

There's just one thing you need to know about love

but the damn dream switched before she could tell

A dream like that is like a joke without a punchline

Your cancer is like a joke without a punchline

Now–I don't know much about love

but I do know two hours parking at the new Adelaide hospital will

  cost you seven bucks

and that some specialists are weird, man

and have no tact.

I wish your tumour was a rare mushroom blooming in a galaxy far
   far away
I want to burrow into it
and blast it with jokes
because we know laughter is the best medicine
But –
we also know my jokes, so –
let's put Catherine Tate
in the Opera House instead
and night after sold-out night I will push her into your penis
so your tumour dissolves into laughter and applause
and that aura of shame you wear like a hoodie will melt away
like Arctic ice.

I don't know if that's possible
I don't know many dead people
I don't know if a man is still a man when he doesn't have a penis
and we don't talk of such things
We are listening instead to that antiseptic urologist
who seems to be saying
Come back next Thursday, mate, and I'll cut off your dick

I rub your back when you're sick in the car park
and that's when you tell me as a kid you slept outside
to feel stars inside you like friends
And when dawn broke and those stars disappeared you wept
because you thought you'd never see them again.

We are gliding the spiral of our Milky Way galaxy
You're alive
and deeper than the darkness descending
And I see now

this is it
this is love.

Resistance

Your eyes glow in the dark like two iPhone 7s
My footsteps are a train track to your heart
You are better than the thing that's better than sliced bread
More precious than rare sandalwood growing in the hot northern
   lands.

You are my Foodland, my shopping list, my Bendigo Bank
You're the squeak in my front gate, the bubbles in my sink
You're my new Smeg oven, my unblocked loo
My shiny clean floor is nothing, *nothing* compared to you.

You're my banana, my apple and guava baby
You're the whole fruit bowl
You're that glow in the Adelaide hills at dawn
And when the day folds you are there in my chair
The comfy red one with the footrest
You are in my bed, babe
You are what comes next.

And even in my dreams I see you
Shooting through the city like a supersonic star
The sky wild and jealous of your brilliance
The sky is jealous of you
The ocean has no depth compared to you
I would not lie about you bcs you are in my teeth
My tongue
My jaw
You are the throbbing of my blood.

And on Sundays when we walk together along the Torrens
Behind that old West End brewery
We can forget about Mondays
And mothers
And mad war-mongering presidents
And the straight lines of this little city
Bcs we are the mystery
                    in the mystery
And we talk about how we love
                    and are loved
So when the world fails us

And people fail us

And we fail each other

And disappoint ourselves

You know what, babe?

We can resist falling

        apart.

Talking Bob Dylan Blues

Jesus, Zimmerman
when did you get so old?
Almost eighty, but the ad on Facebook for your Australian tour
shows a man forty years younger –

Bob Dylan at Budokan 1978

a place where you tried to flee the terrible weight of mysterious
  legend
Watching that footage now makes me feel deflated
Like a flaccid pink balloon, it makes me want to cry.

Wait – did I say that out loud?
Cos you are looking at me like I'm trying to start a fight
The light in here is so much brighter since I changed the bulb
      and your thoughts have wrinkles, man
But, Zimmerman
I am not trying to start a fight
I am trying to come to terms with breaking up with you

When I was twenty-four I couldn't imagine ever wanting to break up
    with you
Man,
When I was twenty-four I fantasised about loving you
In an urban backyard sandpit, haloed by cheap fairy lights,
we shared Winston cigarettes
a bottle of Jack's
and jokes about The Beatles
Now, people will tell you there are all kinds of loving, sweetheart
but you and me know what I'm talking about
don't we, Zimmerman?

Mind you, you're so good at being silent it could go either way
but I am definitely closer to death than I've ever been
and these things were bound to come up
    – loving
    – disappointment
    – not being dead
    – the point in life where you change or cease
When I die I want to be as happy as Brett Whiteley on a good day
with a bunch of violets in my hand

And a sledgehammer and a grain of sand in my head.

Man, I swear the wiring in this room is fucked
the bulb seems to blow every two weeks
Do you remember last December when my demented Mum came to
   visit?
She didn't recognise me in this shadowy room, she said
*You could pass for my daughter, you've got the same eyes but you're
   not my daughter*
I said
Mum, if I'm not your daughter then who the hell am I?
I am no longer the person who fantasises about loving you,
   Zimmerman
I got nothing to say to you
You would just disappoint me I reckon
even though you orbited my twenties like Saturn's rings
even though listening to you was like having no-strings sex with my
   bff
and when I lay on rented lino floors
nursing my complex inferiority in the recovery position for weeks
your music wrapped itself around me like St John crepe.

But that wasn't you, was it?

And I am not me, am I?

They say life is a carnival but, man

are you convinced?

When kids these days trust Facebook more than the government?

And Jesus, Zimmerman, why'd you have to get so old?

It makes me want to cry

I want to go to your concert but I don't want to go to your concert

It'll be winter in Australia

an outside gig in Adelaide's Bonython Park

and I'll complain about my cold feet

and your voice that I once jerked off to will be all out of

                                                    shape

a parody of itself

hard in all the wrong places.

Like an ancient blood-soaked animal found dead on the tracks

I have a limited emotional range

I'm on repeat

afraid of too much

think I might cry again
And tomorrow I will phone Mum
remind her to take her tablets
like I do every morning
and if she's on a good day she will say
Oh, sweetheart
I thought it was you!

Immigration 1973

the day before we flew to Australia we went to Trearddur Bay. my
sister pulled off my wellies and Nain kissed me. the snow was cold
on my tongue. the wind blew Nain's red scarf over the frozen sea.
she said it would meet me in Australia but it never did. the next
morning we got up when it was dark. my breath was like smoke.
Uncle Alan drove us from Bryngwran to Manchester in the rain. the
wipers knocked the rain sideways and wind blew the trees. my sister
held my hand in the back seat. Mum said it was a miserable day to
be going, like all of Wales was crying for us and our leaving. the
light was bright inside the airport, the floor white shiny. we stood
next to people in a zig-zag line longer than a snake. a man stamped
Mum and Dad's passports. he said good luck. our suitcases went on
a conveyer belt and got swallowed up by a black hole. we went to
Gate 58 but there was no gate. my sister held Dad's hand to find us
hot dinners and a cup of tea for Mum. I sat on a glass table top. it
unbalanced and made a loud crashing noise. when Dad came back he
said he heard it from the other side of the airport and knew it was me.
Mum spilt hot tea on the fluffy blue jumper she bought especially. we
had another hot dinner on the plane. I was sick. when I woke up the
air-hostess said I was brave. she had on pink lipstick. after I finished
the colouring-in book I was sick again. I drew a picture of Nain
waving on the shore of Trearddur Bay with the frozen sea behind her.
Dad said the desert was underneath us. it was dark. I couldn't see. it
was dark for a long time. we flew in space next to the moon

Lonely

there is nothing as lonely
as a single bunch of daffodils
discounted
in a blue bucket
drooping
next to the Chupa Chups
on the dirty glass counter
of the Northlakes Plaza
Smoke Shop

600,000

My mother is happy enough
singing Engelbert Humperdinck
lying on the narrow bed
of the nursing home
that she chose last year
that she does not remember choosing

And she's well fed
three square meals a day

with a bottomless bucket of brew in-between

white with one

because she forgot that she drinks it weak black

And she's safe enough

but the drugs prescribed to manage her dementia

make her unsteady

so I hold her hand to cross the road

and her skin, it's softer than I remember

tender, like an old paper bag

used over and over

And people will tell you it's sad

And people will tell you

*Moving your mum into a nursing home is one of the hardest things
    you will ever do*

and it turns out

it's true

but I am grateful

she's not strapped to a chair

so doped up that she can't move

that she doesn't present with maggots in her wounds

or lying for hours in her own shit
because shit regulation means shit nursing homes can stay open
with no penalty
no sanctions
and no obligation to disclose investigations or complaints made
against them

72 reviews into the Aged Care Industry
in the last 11 years and still we're on this treadmill of
      chronic understaffing
      undertraining
      overmedicating
      underregulating
But hey – let's sink $105 million
into a Royal Commission
to find out what needs to be done

And moving right along – it's 2031
and the chances are I've buried my mum
But what are the odds you reckon
that 11 years on from this Royal Commission
all or any of its recommendations

have been actioned?

20 to one?
100 to one?
600,000 to one?

Because in 2031
that's how many people in Australia are living with dementia

600,000

God help us

God help you and yours
Because prayer will bring you more comfort
than Australia's Aged Care laws

Something strange is going on inside the sun

Something strange is going on inside the sun
There's a hole in her centre the size of fifteen hundred Earths
and nobody seems to know what fills that hole
and Margaret, who is that woman in your face?
Something strange is going on inside your face.

And the broccoli grows strange in our garden
leaves wider than the sleeves of a Renaissance gown
but the green heads look demented, deformed
devoured by predators with tiny teeth
and Margaret, I too have become strange.

I think of death and people dying, all the time
I think of lives lost to dementia, all the time
I hear your memories crack and splinter, shards of people
place and time shot through with foggy darkness
and Margaret, I think your memories are filling the hole in the sun.

Here is Bryngwran, the Welsh village you were raised in
Here's your mother, my grandmother
sewing by the light of a candle
Your father tends the garden
Your brother calls you in from the stream
where you swim with your twin sister.

Here are your people who grow things
Here are your people who make things
who sing children out of rain
who sing bones into earth to lay them down again
in the land of your mothers, the land of your fathers.

And that old sun swells with the strangeness
of memory's broken bones
but I am singing them back in this poem
And you can call it selfish
but I am singing them back because I need to remember
who we are in this strangeness we've become
And so I sing.

And I will keep on singing, in sunshine
and in rain and on foggy winter mornings
until you come running, like a child through the fog
to her mother's open arms
Ecstatic to be found at last.

In praise of temporary people

Rabbits wail on moonlit mounds. How much pleasure to cry over and over and pluck-storm the briar together! The queen boldly scrapes her heels along pavements, taming rulers upon the brilliant asphalt. Flowers fall, blooms break darkly. Gallant armies pull down Took Mountain in an igniting opus of blue chime surge while temporary people leak loads of knowledge, find rips and gaps in the kite history of dinosaurs and play solemnly with knives and crates of whisky. Talk now, nocturnal heaven! for nous and pie shun crime in the houses of men.

Last dog

After I had my dog put down I went to the beach where I saw another
black staffy chomping on frothy waves like she was that crazed with
thirst and hunger she could have drunk the ocean, eaten all the fish,
dived to the bottom to feed on crays, munched her way through the
Great Barrier Reef, before gobbling up the entire Pacific trash vortex.
Then a squall of kids stormed out of the Life Savers Club, scaring the
shit out of me in their red rashies, and when the staffy heard them
she took one quick preserving look over her shoulder, plunged into
the sea and paddled like mad. And I remembered my first dog, the
way she took ill suddenly. After the fits you could smell terror on her,
metallic and wet like steel pipes left in the rain and I was that hard
on myself because I got more upset over that dog than my dad, who
had died the previous summer. I'd watched him shrink to half his
size in the hospital bed, wiping grey gunk from his mouth, holding
my breath against foul-smelling boils that erupted on him daily as
if anger were its own revenge. I watched the staffy drift to safety
further up the beach but it did make me think that when the oceans'
fish have dried up, the reefs are white as styrofoam, the purple seas
stink like burning coal and there are only starving mobs of kids left,
this is the way the last dog will go: hounded by a herd of freckle-
heads across blistering sands, she'll be forced to dive beneath toxic
waves before disappearing for good. I sat in the shallows, let sand fill
my knickers, knocked the top off a bottle of bourbon and bawled my
bloody eyes out.

Poem to my younger self

so I said to my younger self, I said – Kiddo
when I was you, a girl who loved to colour in
green was my favourite colour
I remember a green velour dress ribbed at the cuffs and neck
a pair of beautiful green flares that made me feel so grown up
and this bit kinda sucks but
colouring in outside the lines?
that, to me, was freedom.

now, Kiddo
I'm not saying your life's going to be all about green
or colouring in
it's not about being seen in the right places
and the whirlpools of scandal and gossip
who went to which school
who breeds better babies
who got fat first
who drives a Mercedes
it's not about these things

it's not stomping your footprint on the face of the world
or parading your power-heeled-red-dressed businesswoman boldly
   where
no woman has ever gone before – No

it's not Ten Commandments
market forces
globalisation
forging a nation by statistics
logistics
linguistics
and think tanks are for drowning in
it's not seven steps to younger-looking skin

and here's another thing it's not about –
them and those/us and we
it's not always about you
and it's not about me, Kiddo
which brings me back to green

when I was you, a girl who loved to colour in

green was my favourite colour
I remember that green velour dress ribbed at the cuffs and neck
and those beautiful green flares that shook things up
and maybe it's just luck that, for me
colouring in outside the lines
meant freedom

now, I'm not saying your life is going to be all about green
but it might just be about the green house of a wood mouse
offering warmth in a mid-winter frost
or staring for hours at your dog's wrinkled brow
because it helps you to think
forgetting what comes next as you worship at the altar
of poetry's creamy buttocks and say
Darling, I should like to eat you roasted and salted
from the good green bowl we reserve for visitors!

it's the secrets you discover in the slippery strange of words
when the bodyguards of language dissolve

and you will know that you know something

when your shortcomings shudder
to unfurl your mind
until you fizz
with alternative points of view

when the thorns in your side turn into bellyaches
churning guts burning
pathways of change
for others to walk on

hold hands with falling friends, Kiddo
be curious about wombats
know the facility of your backbone
and remember to tear the wound apart
so you can bring back light to illuminate the dark
and sometimes
go back to where you came from and say –
Mother, you are as graceful as a kestrel
on a showcase summer day
as beautiful as that green velour dress
as necessary as heartache

and she may say –

Daughter, when I was a child
I lived by Romance and green dragons
danced to the tune of red robins in the foxgloves
and when I was scared by a big-boned warlock
who appeared suddenly in a boiling sky
I was lucky, Daughter
because a wood mouse offered me her house
and we sped to safety together

and that, Kiddo, was just the beginning.

Lost

most days   i am not a poet

most days   i am lost in the spaces between poems

and when i go looking i don't want to find suffering and regret

but that's the thing about poetry

it can lead you where you don't want to be led

and so

here i am
i'm twelve

i'm quiet as an egg when they said

lindy chamberlain murdered her own child

and it was 32 years before that woman's name was
cleared

i am lost in these spaces/these places

between poems

and some days

(not most days, just some days)

i do regret not doing more when I was younger

all those jobs i didn't strive for

compliments i never paid

books i never read, or wrote

poetry readings

protest marches

family lunches

i missed them bcs i was still pissed from

the night before when i kissed

the wrong boy & had unsafe sex

regrets, right?

i've have a few

but then again

the only one thing i truly regret is

that i didn't listen more

to the wind, shifting

the earth, trembling

and to my heart, that old chestnut

bcs if i had known how to listen

i might have discovered sooner how to trust

getting lost in these spaces/these places

between poems

getting lost in the crook of an arm

or the shadow of a rock

in a stranger's story of suffering

or the whiff of bad luck

in my thoughts

as they fly over sun-drenched roofs disappearing into light

in the palace that is night

and in the astounding silence when we turn off our phones

and listen –

in my lifetime almost 70% of the world's animals have disappeared
bcs of uncontrolled human expansion. there are more displaced
people now than after world war two. the chairman of the board of
the sydney theatre company is also the ceo of the commonwealth
bank

i get lost in these spaces/these places between poems

and when i went searching for an ending

all i could find was this smart-arsed poem

who told me –

you will find your end in the place of grace where poetry is heard

(and there you are)

Acknowledgements

The poems and prose in this book were (mostly) written in the last decade but
some reach further back. During the time of writing I had the support of many
people, organisations and communities. If I knew a Welsh word for thanking a
thousand people but not having enough space in one small book to do so, I would
insert it here. Instead, I've compiled a (relatively) short list:

TO Bronwyn Mehan – brilliant human, publisher and champion of short form
writing and writers in Australia – for saying yes, for the Sydney bed, for putting
together a dream team in less time than it takes to sharpen a pencil, and for all
the rest. To Bettina Kaiser – graphic designer and illustrator extraordinaire – for
the beautifully haunting artwork and for the black holes into which the page
numbers will forever fall; her images make me long for something I didn't know
I'd forgotten. To Matilda Gould, whose wonderful editing eyes saw what I couldn't
and who never said no, or if she did it was with such gentleness, good will and
charm that I never noticed. To Heike Krieger for her magical assistance with
typesetting while out in The Dandenongs. To Susan McCreery, for the top shelf
spit and polish –

diolch.   (thanks)

TO Arts South Australia, Sarah Tooth and the SA Writers Centre (now Writers
SA); Miles Merrill, Word Travels and the Australian Poetry Slam; Kami McInnes,
Daniel Watson and Spoken Word SA. To Donna Ward, Tricia Dearborn, Threasa
Meads, Jennifer Mills, Cate Kennedy, Rosslyn Prosser and Steve Smart for their
generosity, kindness and gentle words of encouragement –

diolch.

TO the members of Darwin Authors Group (DAGS), who gave me feedback on the early pieces and encouraged me to keep going. To the generous folk in the Australian (and especially South Australian) spoken word communities who gave me space, a stage, a mic and an audience –

diolch.

TO my family and friends. To Indigo – unofficial spoken word coach, cheerleader and fellow poet – who understands the power of words (& silence) more than anyone I know. To Seana, who stood in her sunny kitchen and told me Stompy's story; and to Stompy, who allowed me to retell it. To Alysha, who talked to me about the impact of drought on South Australia's Riverland. To Shaine, whose suggestions made 'Something strange' something much better. To Gary, for the title 'Highway One' and for listening to me recite poetry while he repaired my mother's kitchen. To Sarah, for the inspiring afternoons of signing poetry in Auslan in Perth –

diolch.

Biggest thank you of all to Brent, for the laughs and love in the spaces between poems –

    diolch yn fawr, my love.

Credits

Some poems and stories in this book have been performed and/or published and/or adapted into video-poems and/or won prizes and/or nearly won prizes. One was found languishing on a footpath in the rain. Another announced itself at a family wedding. Yet another cheekily popped up in London's West End at a fundraiser for Orchid, the UK's leading charity fighting male cancer. And one of the video-poems travelled the world and was spotted by festivalgoers in Cork, Ireland; George Town, Penang; and Adelaide, Australia. Thank you to all the publishers, editors, directors, filmmakers, producers, organisers, and other lovely people responsible for the first publication, selection and promotion of these works:

'Murder Girl gets wired' – published in *Indigo Vol 1* by Tactile Books 2007

'A Ceremony to Commemorate the Golden Jubilee of Queen Elizabeth II' – published in *fourW twenty New Writing* by fourW press; and commended in The Booranga Prize 2009

'Bella's Wedding' – published in *Indigo Vol 4* by Tactile Books 2009

'Cooked Bones' – published in *Indigo Vol 6* by Tactile Books, and *Bruno's Song* by NT Writers' Centre 2011

'Ollie's Blood Roses' – second prize in the Boroondara Literary Awards 2011

'Highway One' – published by *Verity La* 2012

'Satisfied' – performed at *Spineless Wonders Presents* and *Little Fictions* 2012

'Cultural Submissions' – published by *Verity La* 2013

'Just for Jesus' – published in *apt* by Aforementioned Productions, Inc. USA 2013

'Who Likes Custard?' – published in *Stoned Crows & other Australian icons* by Spineless Wonders 2013

'Colonisation' – published by *Seizure Online* 2014

'One Blue Eye' – published in *Flashing the Square* by Spineless Wonders 2014

'Activism' – finalist in SA Poetry Slam 2016

'Resistance' – finalist in SA Poetry Slam 2017

'the kid' – published in *fourW twenty-eight: New Writing* by fourW press 2017

'Last Dog' – shortlisted in Bath Flash Fiction Award UK 2017

'Being human' – finalist in Australian Poetry Slam 2018

'Lost' – winner of Draw Your (S)words Poetry Slam 2017; adapted into a video-poem by director Pamela Boutros and shortlisted in the Ó Bhéal Poetry-Film competition 2019

'Stars' – winner of Goolwa Poetry Cup 2019

'To Touch & Taste a Comet' – published by *Cordite Poetry Review* 2018; adapted into a video-poem by director Patrick Zoerner 2019

'this little poem' extract in *Raining Poetry in Adelaide* street-festival by University of Adelaide and the J M Coetzee Centre for Creative Practice 2019

'Something strange is going on inside the sun' – runner-up in SA Poetry Slam 2019

'600,000' – winner of Zest Fest Senior Slam 2019; finalist in Australian Poetry Slam 2019; adapted into a video-poem by director Pamela Boutros 2019

Find Caroline:
Blog: carolinereidwrites.blogspot.com
Facebook: facebook.com/carolinereidpoet
Instagram: instagram.com/caroline.reid.writes
Vimeo: vimeo.com/carolinereidpoet
Twitter: twitter.com/caroline__reid

www.ingramcontent.com/pod-product-compliance
Lightning Source LLC
Chambersburg PA
CBHW082122180726

48291CB00011B/2812